W9-CPV-933

Lacy's Journey
The Life of a Decorator Crab

Story and Illustrations by
Loretta Halter

Music by
Steve Halter

Published by
Nature's Hopes & Heroes
Boulder Creek, California

ACKNOWLEDGEMENTS

I wish to give special thanks to John Tucker Osgood, my husband, friend, and editor, for his constant support, insight, dedication to, and belief in my work. My deepest appreciation also goes to Steve Halter, my brother, for the love and magic he poured into composing and performing the music for my story. I want to express my thanks to Mom and Dad for their support and use of their home for a studio. I wish to give thanks to Mark Ricciardi, from Angel M. Studios, who mixed and mastered the music for my book. Great thanks goes to Jim Mullen and to his apprentice Virginia Gavel, designers and consultants, who worked closely and enthusiastically with me on this book, as well as my first story, *A Voice for the Redwoods*. I also wish to thank Kristen Jacobson for helping me patiently with the early preparations of *Lacy's Journey*. Lastly, I wish to give thanks to all the environmental organizations who work so hard to protect and preserve our oceans, for future generations to enjoy and cherish.

Publisher:

Nature's Hopes and Heroes
www.natureshopesandheroes.com
Boulder Creek, California

ISBN: 978-0-9822942-1-5

Printed on Recycled Paper

Special Notes: 10% of the author's proceeds from the sale of this book will be donated to environmental organizations.

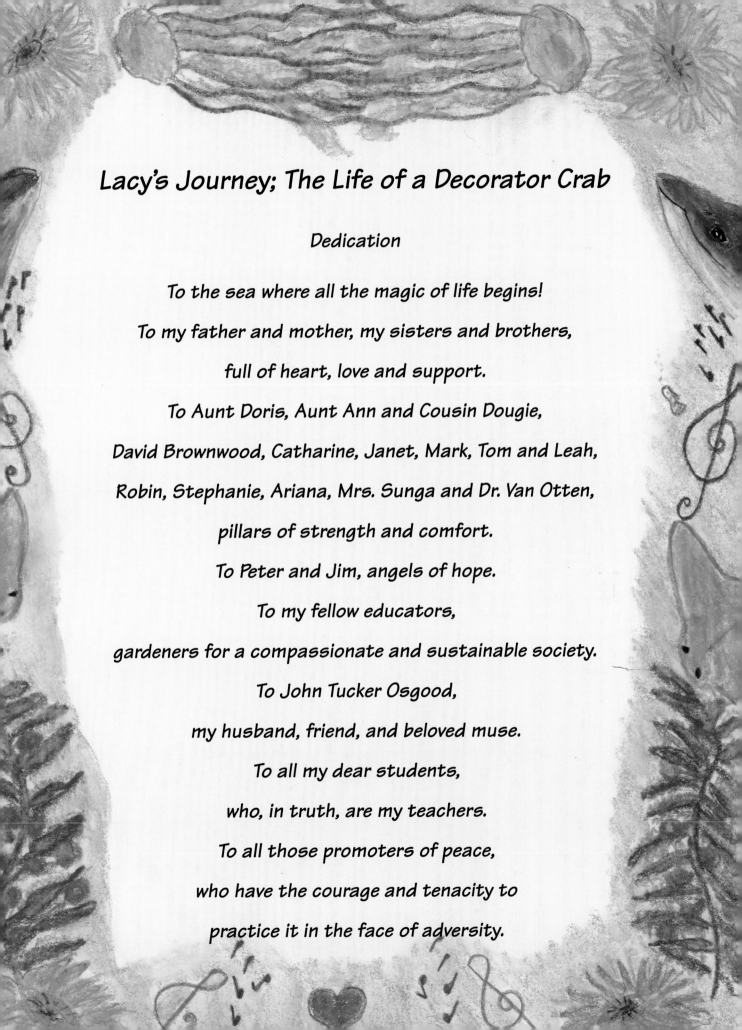

Lacy's Journey; The Life of a Decorator Crab

Dedication

To the sea where all the magic of life begins!

To my father and mother, my sisters and brothers,

full of heart, love and support.

To Aunt Doris, Aunt Ann and Cousin Dougie,

David Brownwood, Catharine, Janet, Mark, Tom and Leah,

Robin, Stephanie, Ariana, Mrs. Sunga and Dr. Van Otten,

pillars of strength and comfort.

To Peter and Jim, angels of hope.

To my fellow educators,

gardeners for a compassionate and sustainable society.

To John Tucker Osgood,

my husband, friend, and beloved muse.

To all my dear students,

who, in truth, are my teachers.

To all those promoters of peace,

who have the courage and tenacity to

practice it in the face of adversity.

Whale Song

Hatched from an egg only hours ago, a tiny decorator crab ventured into her new world. There was only one thing that prevented her from being invisible: her two large eyes. Her eyes were wide open with curiosity as she looked all around. She was floating on the surface of the sea with millions of other tiny plankton, and what a hungry bunch they were! All of them were feasting on diatoms, sea plants that were just a little smaller than these sea creatures. You might think that is tiny, but to the plankton, these diatoms were quite large. Imagine if you tried to eat a carrot or an apple nearly as large as yourself!

The diatoms were delicious to eat, so crunchy and sweet, but to the tiny crab they were also beautiful. They glistened in the sun like thousands of tiny rainbow colored diamonds. She wanted to dress herself with these jewels of the sea, but just as she reached out to hold a diatom, two giant shadows moved swiftly overhead. Then the larger of the two giants opened its mouth wide. Against her will, the crab felt herself being pulled towards the monstrous creature. Just ahead of her she could see thousands of tiny plankton being sucked in and trapped between long, fibrous strands that hung down from inside the monster's mouth. She was only inches away from being sucked in when the giant suddenly shifted directions, causing her to slam against a small barnacle right next to the monster's jawbone. She scrambled inside the barnacle for protection. She wondered how she could possibly escape.

The two Goliaths traveled on for what seemed like ages to the little crab. She knew something large was trailing close behind by the loud, haunting cries that followed until the waters grew dark. She crouched down inside the barnacle, shivering with fear until she finally fell asleep.

—◆—

Hours later, she woke with a start. She peeked outside her hiding place, hungry. A few diatoms drifted by, which she greedily snatched up and ate. She looked about her and noticed the waters growing steadily lighter, but she felt an oppressive silence surround her as she considered how far away she must be from where she belonged. Her whole body began to tremble until the larger of the two creatures began to sing very softly.

> *Come with me, Baby,*
> *my little humpback whale,*
> *Together we'll travel,*
> *Far away we shall sail,*
> *To the deep, hidden seas*
> *Where mysteries abound,*
> *Where you'll grow and swim freely,*
> *With love all around.*
> *Come with me, Baby,*
> *My little humpback whale,*
> *Together we'll travel,*
> *Far away we shall sail,*
> *You will learn how to sing,*
> *To the rhythms of the waves*
> *To the tides and the seasons*
> *The earth always brings.*
> *Come with me, Baby,*
> *My little humpback whale,*
> *Together we'll travel,*
> *Far away we shall sail,*
> *You will take my love with you*

No matter how far,
I will guide and protect you
Like a shining night star,
My love will be with you,
Like a shining night star.

As the tiny decorator crab listened to the mother whale sing to her calf, she felt a sense of peace come over her. Yet it was mingled with sadness. She forgot her own fears and without thinking, let out a sigh and murmured, "How beautiful."

The great whale was so surprised that she swung her whole body around trying to find where the voice had come from. "Who are you that speaks?"

The tiny decorator crab shivered, wishing she had never said anything. If she spoke, would this monstrous creature figure out where she was hiding and eat her? But somehow, as the whale's song echoed in her mind, her fears abated. "I am…just a little decorator crab. I am…I was…afraid…to speak with you, but somehow your song made me think of my own mother. I never got to know her. She died not long after I was born, and yet your song made me feel as if she was with me."

"I am sure she is still with you," said the whale in reassuring tones. "You have shown great courage to speak your heart to me, but have no fear. I have no intention of eating you. Instead, we must return you to your own home so you can keep growing."

The little crab felt relief and joy. "How can I thank you enough?"

"I feel your appreciation, and that is enough for me, little crab. So where are you hiding, anyway?"

"I am here, inside this old, abandoned barnacle, very close to your mouth."

"Ah, of course! That explains it!"

"What?"

"The reason I hear you so well is because my ears are located right next to my jawbone where that old barnacle is." The musical tones in her voice almost carried a sound like laughter, as she swung her great body around. The little crab observed how gracefully the baby calf was able to follow his mother. Then to the crab's surprise, the calf swam as close as he could get to the barnacle to have a better look at the tiny crab. Then as soon as it made eye contact with her, he cried out excitedly, "Lacy! Lacy, like krill." Then he did a somersault in the water, as if to show off.

"Hmm. 'Lacy.' That is a good name for you, pretty, like all the plankton in sunlit waters."

The little crab was delighted. She felt she was making two new friends. "When your baby speaks, it's almost like a song."

"Yes," the mother whale responded proudly. "Vibrato is still learning, but eventually he will sing, and whistle and chirp all the time."

"Sing? Like you?"

"Indeed, he will be able to sing far better than I."

"But…but you sing so beautifully. I've never heard such a lovely song in my life!"

"My dear Lacy, I'm pleased you got to hear the song I meant only for my own child to hear. In the world of the humpback whales, the males are the true singers. I hope someday you will be able to hear them. Perhaps you heard the one that was following me yesterday. Oh such grand voices they have! One of the reasons they sing is to catch the attention of us females, and it works. I fell in love with Vibrato's father not so long ago."

"Was that Vibrato's father? Where is he now?"

"He is gone. He will not be able to rejoin us again," the mother whale replied weakly.

Lacy suddenly heard a low, sad tone coming from Vibrato. She felt anxious to understand, but wondered if it would hurt her friends if she pressed her for answers. "Maybe I could help you find him? I know I'm small, but I have good eyes."

"He died, little one. Human hunters killed him. Each year humans have killed several whales during our long journey to Alaska."

"But…why?"

"Humans kill to eat, just as every animal must do to survive. The only difference is that humans, unlike other creatures, tend to take more than they need."

Lacy wanted to cry out in low tones with Vibrato.

"I was bitter against humans for a long time until I came to understand that not all humans are the same. Last year I was rescued by one after I got all tangled in a large fishing net, a trap meant for catching smaller fish. The human patiently cut into the cords that held me bound without even hurting me. The voice from this human was so warm and soothing. I never felt so grateful, not just for my life but for what I learned from this experience. I have come to believe that hunger, fear, and the need to survive, govern most of our actions, but when our needs are met, we are able to rise above those forces and extend kindness to others around us, no matter who they are."

The little decorator crab pondered the mother's words. She was still too young to grasp the depth of the whale's belief, yet somehow she knew it was important to keep these words in her heart.

The mother whale headed closer to the surface of the water. Lacy could not see Vibrato, but she could hear him making great splashing sounds overhead. A swarm of tiny plankton, like herself, mixed with lovely diatoms drifted by. The little crab shivered, remembering how the great whale had engulfed thousands of these creatures before. She wondered if the mother whale was hungry again, but the whale continued to swim on, only she slowed down her pace.

"You must be hungry, little crab. I will linger here for a time while you replenish yourself."

"Aren't you going to eat? Aren't you hungry too?"

"You, Lacy, were almost part of my last meal. Once I return to Alaska, I shall have a great feast with my fellow humpbacks. I am looking forward to being with them again."

"Alaska must be close by then."

"No, it is quite a distance from here. It will take us about three months before we arrive."

"But, won't you get hungry?"

"My, yes! By the time we reach Alaska's waters, I will be famished. But until then, I will wait, for that is the way of us whales."

"Oh," Lacy said, stuffing her mouth with a particularly tasty diatom. But suddenly she felt too full to eat another bite. The little crab felt her whole body grow swollen and tight with discomfort. She panicked, wondering if she ate something that was not good for her. She dragged herself back inside the safety of the barnacle, and groaned, "I don't feel good, Mother Whale."

"Just rest. You will be fine in no time. You are just growing up. Your body is going through changes."

Lacy felt her body become increasingly tight. She felt miserable, but the low hum coming from the mother whale soothed her. Then, slowly, Lacy's body began to molt. She wriggled herself free from the old skin and watched it drift off. She was still in her larval state, only a bit larger than before, but now her body felt soft, light and wonderfully free. She felt so giddy she wanted to swim about like her whale companions. But it was as if the mother whale was reading her mind, gently warning her that she was particularly vulnerable in her new body.

"Be patient and stay inside the barnacle for a while longer. Your body will toughen up in time. But take heart, we are close to your place of birth, your home."

As soon as the mother spoke these words, the giddy lightness that Lacy had felt just moments before, seemed to dissolve. She knew she should feel glad, but sadness crept over her.

"Oh, Lacy, what a glorious morning it is. Look up. Can you see the streams of golden light dancing between the giant kelp vines?"

"Yes! How beautiful! Where is it coming from?"

"The sun!" Vibrato cried out joyfully. He propelled himself closer to the surface, and suddenly disappeared. Then an instant later he came crashing back down in the water.

"Where did you go?
How did you do that?"
"It's called 'breaching'
little friend. Sometimes
we just can't resist
leaping for joy for just
being alive!"
"Oh! Teach me how!"
"It isn't good for
you to be exposed
to air for long.
You weren't made
for that."
"I wish I were a
whale! I could
leap and sing and
I could...I could..."
The little crab felt
her heart breaking
inside. She knew her
two friends would
soon leave her behind.
"Lacy, you may not be a
whale, but you have the heart
of one! Hold on as tight as you

8

can to the barnacle. Are you ready?"

She braced herself in her barnacle. "I'm ready."

"Here we go!"

Using her powerful tail and flippers, the mother whale picked up speed as she propelled herself upward. Then suddenly she breached the surface of the water! The little decorator crab felt a rush of excitement as she soared high above the water along side the great whale. She could also see Vibrato, nearby! Nearly his entire body rose above the ocean's surface, and then he did a backward flip into the water. She glimpsed the reflection of the sun on the water before she and Mother Whale plunged back in to the sea.

The mother whale swam close to a rocky area just below the low tide-line. "Here is your home, Lacy."

The little crab stayed inside the barnacle, but remained silent.

"Lacy, you have the great heart of a whale, though you are small. As a decorator crab, you have your own special gifts that you will recognize as you grow. You have only been with me for a couple of days, yet you are like a daughter to me and as such, I must insist that you come out. You cannot survive the journey Vibrato and I must take. I want you to grow strong and healthy so that we can see you again when we return again next year. Come out, and move further up the rocks. I wish to give you something before we leave."

Lacy reluctantly left the barnacle shell and, using her feathery fronds, she swam up the rocks above her whale mother. For the next twenty minutes, she watched as the huge whale rubbed back and forth, back and forth against a sharp rock that protruded out of the rock face. What was she doing? Then suddenly she saw the old barnacle float slowly up towards her. It caught on the edge of a small rock just an inch away from where she stood.

"Your body is going to undergo so much change, we won't be able to recognize you. This barnacle is too large for you to wear right now, but you will grow."

"Thank you, Mother Whale. I will treasure it as long as I live. And as soon as I grow big enough, I will wear it and remember you."

"See you next year, my daughter."

"See you next year, sister whale-crab," Vibrato sang. His voice filled her with hope and strength as she watched the two sail off.

Lessons

Three weeks had passed since Lacy had watched her two friends sail off for Alaska. Her body continued to grow and molt. Tiny arms with claws replaced the feathery fronds she used to have. Lacy found that her new claws were quite useful for picking up all kinds of plants and animals smaller than herself. She was still much too tiny to wear the abandoned barnacle that the mother humpback whale had given to her, but she took comfort in the refuge it provided her. Yet, at the same time, the barnacle reminded her of her loneliness. It would be several months before her two whale friends would return.

"Well, it's about time I start making new friends," she told herself. She began searching for tiny crab larvae like herself, but after a week passed, her efforts appeared unsuccessful. "Just be patient, and stop feeling sorry for yourself, Lacy," she scolded. Then she made up her mind to get to know the other types of sea creatures living around her. There were so many to choose from in the kelp beds near the rocky shoreline. There were round, spiky, purple sea urchins, a variety of sea stars, some with an amazing amount of arms. There were schools of bat rays: the flying creatures of the sea that whirled below her before she could catch their attention and say, "Hi!" She didn't know where or how to strike up a conversation with any of the strangers of the sea until she caught sight of two sea otter pups wrestling with each other. They nearly knocked her over as they darted by, but just in time, Lacy grabbed hold of a single frond from the kelp bed and hung on tight. From her newfound vantage point she could see other otters grooming themselves, while others were feeding on sea urchins, shellfish, and, "Oh," she shivered. The one who was closest to her was eating a large crab. Lacy was about to turn away and consider making friends with a more suitable companion, but curiosity got the better of her. "Besides," she told herself, "Mother Whale could have eaten me, but she didn't. And...and didn't she tell me that when hunger needs are met, that creatures can be kind?" Lacy eyed the sated otter, and observed how carefully she bathed and preened herself. The otter first rolled over and over in the water to get all the food scraps and shells off her. Next, she pressed her forepaws against her fur to get excess water out. She rubbed herself fastidiously, and blew on herself to get her fur more fluffy and dry. "Ooohh, nice and clean, now," Lacy thought to herself. But then she caught sight of one, very tiny piece of algae that was caught in the otter's fur. Apparently, the otter hadn't noticed that it was right underneath her chin. Abandoning all caution, Lacy released the kelp frond and drifted on over to the otter and clambered on top of its belly. "Hold perfectly still," Lacy ordered.

"What?"

"I said, 'HOLD STILL.'" Lacy reached up and grabbed the sticky piece of algae and gave it a quick yank. "There!"

"Ouch! What did you do that for?"

"See?" Lacy proudly held up the piece of algae. "You missed a spot when you were cleaning yourself. Now you look perfect! And gosh, your fur is so soft!"

"Uh...I guess I should, um...thank you, but...Hey! You are a, well you're almost a crab! You might be puny, but I could eat you, you know! One quick swallow, and you're history."

"Do otters eat whales?" Lacy asked boldly.

"No. Of course not. That's not part of our diet."

"Well then, you won't want to eat me because I am a whale-crab."

"Oh," the otter replied, dumbfounded.

"My name is Lacy. Mother Whale named me. What's your name?"

"My name is Sierra."

"I noticed that nearly all the otters wrestle with each other or chase each other. Why is that?"

"I guess whale-crabs don't know what play is?"

Lacy looked at Sierra quizzically. "Play?"

"Huh! I bet you're just an ordinary crab!"

"Ah, come on. Just give me a chance," Lacy pleaded.

"Well…alright," she answered impatiently. "We chase each other and wrestle just for fun." Lacy looked puzzled but said nothing. "Just what I thought. You have a lot to learn about the right way to live!"

"Does that mean you're going to teach me?" Lacy asked excitedly.

For a moment, it seemed that Sierra's eyes lit up with amusement, but her voice remained cool. "One of the biggest rules that otters live by is to not do anything unless it is fun," she said matter of factly.

"Oh! Like when Mother Whale carried me with her as she leaped for joy out of the water! That was the most thrilling experience I have ever had."

"Well, that's a good start," Sierra nodded approvingly. "But what about playing games?"

"No," she replied sheepishly.

"Humph! It's about time you learn how to live right. Playing for the sheer pleasure and excitement it gives is part of what makes life worth living. Take the game of tag, for instance. Now, let me tell you how my own mama taught me, and her mama before that told her how to play tag, and before that, how my great grandma taught my grandma so that my mom could learn. But even before that…"

"Umm. You mean you have a bunch of grandmothers?"

"Oh, never mind all that. Just pay attention to how you play the game."

"You tell her, girl," another otter said as she popped her head out of the water.

"Yeah. I'd sure like to know how you intend to explain tag to a shrimp of a crab like that."

"Think you can do better than me, Bobby?" Sierra teased back.

"Oh, I wouldn't dream of interfering," Bobby said testily. "And neither would Fronda. Isn't that right, Fronda?"

"Certainly not. But, if you need us to demonstrate, we will gladly cooperate."

"Nosy rascals. Don't you agree, Lacy?"

Lacy began to understand the spirit of play. "Yes. Very nosy rascals."

Bobby and Fronda looked at Lacy with surprise, looked at each other, and back at Lacy.

"Impressed, are you? You should be," Sierra said smugly. "This is no ordinary 'shrimp of a crab.' This is Lacy."

"I'm definitely impressed," said Fronda. "Lacy, huh? What kind of a crab are you?"

"I'm a whale-crab."

"Well. I ain't impressed yet. If she can learn to play tag, then she might just earn my respect. But I ain't holding my breath."

Three more otters came up to see what was going on, while Sierra looked Lacy squarely in the eyes. "You ready, Lacy?"

Lacy looked around at her growing audience. Her heart was racing, her body was trembling, but she wasn't about to let Sierra down. Then, in that moment, it seemed like a miracle occurred. From out of nowhere, a sense of determination came over her.

"I am ready to learn," she said confidently.

Fronda swam up right next to Sierra, and looked at the very tiny crab on Sierra's tummy. "Of course you're ready, and you will do just fine," she whispered. She disappeared into the water, but then reappeared just a little ways off.

"To play tag," Sierra started. *"Listen carefully, Lacy."*
"You've got to wiggle, and to squiggle and to
turn around.
You've got to glide and to slide, and to
bob up and down.
Ya' got to be tricky, yes sneaky,
and not make a sound.
You've got to be quick, pull their tail,
without being found.
If they catch ya', they'll get ya', and off
they'll be bound.
And so the game goes,
around and around."

Sierra looked intently at Lacy. "You got it?"

"Let me see if I got this right. 'You've got to...wiggle and to...squiggle, and to, turn around,'" Lacy started slowly.

Suddenly the other otters chimed in and echoed her, but with a lot more rhythm.

"You've got to glide, and to...slide, and to, to, to...Oh! I got it! To bob up and down!"

Once again all the otters started echoing Lacy, bobbing up and down as they spoke. Well, all the otters except, Sierra. She was holding perfectly still. She seemed to be holding her breath.

"Ya' got to be tricky, yes sneaky, and not make a sound," Lacy continued more steadily. As the other otters chimed in, she realized her rhythm was beginning to match theirs. Then she began to mimic the otters' behavior, and bob up and down as she recited the next line.

"Ya' got to be quick! Pull their tail, without being found!"

Then the otters began the next line, "But, if they catch ya..."

"They'll get ya! And off they'll be bound!" Lacy joined in.

"And so the game goes around and around," she finished.

"And so the game goes, around and around," they repeated.

The otters applauded Lacy, even Bobby. Fronda swam up close once more. "I knew you could do it, Lacy!" Then she suddenly let out a yelp and vanished. One of the otters had pulled her tail.

Sierra beamed at Lacy, then looked out at the otters as they played. She was unaware that Lacy tiptoed down towards Sierra's tail, and then gave it a quick tug with her claw, and slipped underneath, to hide between thick kelp fronds.

Transitions

Two weeks had passed, and Lacy had become an accepted playmate of Sierra's group. She felt happy to be among such a jovial bunch. But with her growing body, came growing concerns that she tried to ignore. Just the other day, Lacy felt a strong urge to dress herself with deep green algae. She just started attaching some to her carapace, when Sierra gently reprimanded her, since Sierra took pride in how well she had trained Lacy to clean herself. But this wasn't her only nagging concern.

Lacy appreciated how thoughtful and protective Sierra became of her whenever her body started to molt, but there was an unsettling fear that soon she would lose her tail. She knew that would mean she wouldn't be able to swim. Instead her body would grow heavier and heavier, and sink to the bottom. She wondered if the otters would still want to play with her, or if she would even be able to play any more. She also worried over her friend, Sierra, who had become more subdued, especially when her otter friends teased her about being "such a good mom."

One day, Lacy crawled softly onto Sierra's belly, and started helping her preen her luxurious fur. Suddenly a dark shadow passed overhead. She saw a look a of terror sweep across Sierra's face. Lacy turned her body around and looked up. A large eagle was swooping down towards them at great speed. The great bird's talons were outstretched, and just as Lacy saw the deadly claws come close, her body was suddenly yanked down under water in a tight embrace. Sierra swam quite a distance before she was willing to come up again, and even then, she poked her head out of the water very cautiously. "Oh Lacy! If anything happened to you, I...I...don't know what I would do."

Sierra was trembling.

Lacy snuggled as close to Sierra as she could. A warmth of gratitude washed over her, but words seemed caught in her throat. The two of them remained silent for a long time as they watched the glowing pink sun sink behind the fog in the distance. Sierra looked pensively at Lacy, considering her words. Then, at last she spoke.

"Lacy, I have a confession to make."

"What is it?"

Sierra paused, still considering her words. "I don't know how to begin exactly, but, well…okay. This is it. Two years ago, I got pregnant, but my body wasn't ready yet to have a pup. I was too young to carry a healthy baby, so it died. I was so grieved over the loss of my baby that I never wanted a baby again, until…until you came along. You brought joy to my life that I never dreamed would be possible, especially coming from a crab! A whale-crab," Sierra quickly corrected herself. "Anyway, the male otters are coming around again. I'm not sure when exactly they will come, yet I know it will be soon. Those rascally creatures! They love to sneak up on us lady otters and surprise us. But I know now, I am ready. I want to raise a pup of my own. But, I don't want to leave you either. I know this must sound all very confusing to you, because…because it is! I'm one mixed-up otter."

"You sure are," Lacy teased back. "But then, so am I. So, now that you made your confession, it's my turn."

Sierra looked at her curiously.

"Sooo, you know my body is changing…"

"Sooo?"

"So, well, I'm not really a whale-crab." Lacy suddenly felt hot with shame for lying, but Sierra said nothing. "You have every right to eat me right now." She paused, covered her eyes with her two claws, waiting for Sierra to take a chomp. Nothing happened.

"I know there is more to your confession, Lacy. I'm waiting."

"Yeah, well, Mother Whale called me that, but I am…I am just an ordinary decorator crab. And pretty soon, I am going to lose my tail, and I won't be able to swim or move as easily as I do now. I don't even know if I will be able to play anymore. And then, I just can't help myself, I just want to pick the most beautiful sponges, anemones, and algae and let them grow like a garden on my body. But, then," she continued miserably, "if I give in to my crazy impulses, even if you're not too disgusted with the idea of being friends with me, a messy crab, when you come back later on to introduce your pup to me, you won't even recognize me. Why can't things just stay the same?"

"Lacy, Lacy," sighed Sierra, "Why you *are* just as crazy as I am, aren't you? But let me at least set you straight on a couple of things. First and foremost, you are no ordinary crab! I'm sure you earned the name, 'Whale-Crab,' for a good reason. Did Mother Whale tell you why she gave you that title?"

"Yes," Lacy said softly. "She said it was because I had the heart of a whale."

"I don't know much about whales, but I do know that they are creatures of honor, so you were rightfully named. But, you are even more than that! From here on I declare you, 'Whale-Otter Crab' since now you're a part otter too. Here's proof." Sierra shook her head so vigorously that she began to shed a few loose hairs. They softly drifted down on top of Lacy and stuck to her carapace. "There," Sierra said with satisfaction. "Now, as for your losing your tail, I'm surprised a whale-otter crab like you is going to let a small thing like that stop you from playing. Once anyone tastes the joys of play, it gets in to the blood and never dies. You got it, Lacy."

After hearing Sierra's words, Lacy felt such a lightness overtake her. She attempted to breach the waters but instead she fell backwards into the water with a splash. Sierra jumped in after her to play, but then the two of them caught sight of a small group of otters approaching them from a distance. The one in the lead caught Sierra's attention. He was particularly handsome with his thick, dark brown fur. Lacy wasn't sure, but he seemed to be grinning right at Sierra.

Lacy gently tugged Sierra's tail. The two of them broke the surface of the water. She knew her friend was nervous and excited. "Good luck, Sierra."

Sierra kissed Lacy with her nose before Lacy hopped onto the nearest kelp frond. "Thanks, Lacy."

Lacy waved good-bye, then reattached Sierra's hairs just a little more carefully before she headed for the rock piling. She crawled up to her barnacle, tried to squeeze inside, but was just a tiny bit too big now. "Hmm," she mused, "A little longer, and I'll be able to wear that old treasure." She hunkered down close to her barnacle as she thought about the grandness of life around her.

"The sweetness of life,
Full of mystery and fun,
The greatness of friends,
My heart has been won.
Have I any enemies?
I'm not sure if there's one.
But if ill will exists,
Let me not run.
Instead let me stay open
And warm like the sun."

Lacy's gruff, unwhale-like voice, trailed off into a deep and peaceful sleep, unaware that someone close by had heard her song.

Freedom

Lacy's body began molting again, and just as she had predicted, her tail dropped off. She watched as the current carried it far away. Then suddenly a stronger wave rolled through, taking her along and depositing her into a large, fairly deep tide pool. Lacy was anxious to know how far she was from the rock piling that held her barnacle. She crawled towards the edge of the pool and looked out. Just above the tide pool, there were strange, shiny objects strewn all about on the rocky surface along with bits of rotting fish and other smelly foods she couldn't identify. Amidst all these things, only a few feet away, was a large gray and white bird, struggling to free itself from a strange creature that Lacy had never seen before. The creature was nearly transparent, and so thin, Lacy felt sure that the large bird could easily break free from its hold, but after awhile, she began to realize that it was stronger than it looked. It had a firm grip around the bird's neck and beak, yet this six-ringed creature made no attempt to consume its prey. The bird grew weaker with each effort to free itself, and finally seemed to give up. When it lay down on its side, Lacy could no longer stand to see it suffer. She darted out towards the bird, crawled towards its beak, and took a firm hold of the ring that pinned the bird's beak down to its neck. She clamped down on the ring with her claws, and pulled on it until the ring snapped. Then she quickly yanked the ring off the bird and tossed it to the ground. The bird remained motionless, but she could hear it faintly breathing. She waited anxiously over the bird. "Come on," she murmured. "You can make it."

A wave broke over the rocks submerging the two of them briefly and then rolled back. The cold, salty water caused the bird to stir at last. It seemed dazed for only a brief while, but then it tottered unsteadily to its feet, stretched out its neck, and flapped its wings and folded them neatly back in place. Then it looked down to study its emancipator. "Well, I'll be ding-dang-donged. I thought I was just dreaming! But there it still is. A pipsqueak of a crab actually bothered to save its predator. Must be a crazy lunatic."

Lacy wasn't sure what a 'crazy lunatic' was, but she guessed it had something to do with being a fool. Quickly, she gathered her wits. "I probably am a 'crazy lunatic,' but what a waste to see such a great bird die in the jaws of such a cruel creature. How did it get you?"

"The crab called me 'great?' Well, I'll be ding-dong-dang-doodlelied. It must not be that big of a crazy lunatic to recognize a great bird when it sees one. Huh. Well, uh…actually, little Luna, I'm not all that great." The bird suddenly appeared crestfallen. "If I was so great, I would have never got myself trapped in that garbage! I should have listened to my mother when she warned me as a youngster to stay clear of those rings left by humans. She told me a good many horror stories about the various kinds of trash humans tend to leave behind. I didn't take her seriously. I was more interested in getting the food the humans discarded. I was pecking away happily at the delicious morsels, not paying any attention to the rings that were surrounding small chunks of fish. Then, all of a sudden, I really don't know how I managed to scoop up the ring-thing and get it around my neck. It just happened so fast."

"Oh, how dreadful!" Lacy exclaimed.

"Well, if you ask me, it was dumb of me to get myself in that mess in the first place."

"But you were hungry. Sometimes its hard to think clearly when you haven't eaten for a while," Lacy said sympathetically. She looked around desperately for some food to give it, but he spotted some before she did.

"Aha! There is still a piece of dead fish right behind you! You don't see any rings hiding around it do you?"

Lacy inspected the area around the fish carefully. "It's safe."

"Well, dong-dang-ding-doodlely-do!" He snatched up the piece of fish and wolfed it down.

Lacy looked around for more food and found another piece of terrible-smelling fish. She turned to look at him unsure whether it was safe enough to eat. "Here's another piece of fish, but I think it may be too rotten to eat."

"Too rotten to eat? Nonsense! We seagulls are scavengers. It goes against our highest morals to let any kind of food go to waste."

"Oh," Lacy said, both surprised and embarrassed. She did not want to insult him. "Here," she said quickly, finding a small rotting fish that she dragged up to him. She watched with fascination as he downed the fish whole.

"Ding-dang-donged-doodlely-do-be-do, I can't believe it, but it's true! I'm saying thanks to a crab, not only for saving my life, but also for trying to make me feel better. Better pinch me, Luna, with those claws of yours so I can be sure I'm not still just dreaming."

Amused by her new friend, she reached up and plucked at his right webbed foot.

"Ouch! Yep, you're real. I'm not just dreaming."

"My name is Lacy. What's yours?"

"Seymour T. Seagull. I am honored and quite relieved to meet you, Lacy Luna."

"I hate to part company with you so soon, Seymour T. Seagull. There is something I want to ask you: something I don't understand, but I'm feeling a bit dizzy. I've got to return to the tide pool quickly. I need to be in water."

"Well, I'll be do-be-do-doodlely-dong-dang-dinged! A crazy Lacy Luna crab actually wanting to spend time with a dangerous enemy! You must be hungry too, 'cause it's obvious that you're not thinking clearly! And for some crazy reason, I, Seymour T. Seagull, want to help you feel better. What's this world coming to?" With that, Seymour took her gently in his beak, hopped close to the edge of the tide pool, and released her.

Once in the water, she immediately began to tear some sweet red algae to eat. Meanwhile, Seymour T. Seagull patiently waited for her, but he seemed to watch her with equal intrigue, especially when she attached a piece of algae to her carapace that she had nearly finished nibbling on.

She crawled closer to him, keeping herself just under the surface of the water.

"Thanks for waiting for me. I know it takes me a bit longer to eat than you."

"That's for dooong-long-a-ling-sure. But there is no need for thanks. You had a question for me, and I have one for you, so you're keeping me here in a state of curiosity."

"Well, I'll be ding-dang-donged," Lacy responded. "Now you got me in a state of curiosity! I've never had anyone ask me a question. So, don't hold me in suspense anymore. What do you want to know?"

"Why, for dong-ding-dang-doodlely-do-be-do-be-day, do you wear your own food?"

"Well, I...um. I've never given it much thought. It's just what, we decorator crabs do. But, I assure you, it has a practical value to it. You see, suppose I didn't happen to be near any food source, and became really hungry. Like, well, see? When I came to help you, I didn't come well prepared, or stocked with food to help me in an emergency, so you had to help me right away."

"Hmm. That makes sense. Okay. But is that it?"

Lacy thought and thought. In the far recesses of her mind, she heard distant voices calling to her, as if all her ancestors from countless generations ago were trying to tell her something important. It was a single word. "Cam-ou-flage," she said very slowly.

"Of course! Camouflage. Now that makes perfect sense. I should have known that! Most all creatures share that ability to greater or lesser degrees," Seymour T. Seagull said matter-of-factly. Lacy grew silent. She didn't know what the word 'camouflage' even meant, but she was too ashamed to tell Seymour T. Seagull.

"Lacy Luna. Lacy. Ding-dang-ding-a-ling-dong. Is there something wrong? You tired or, or what is it? Hey! And didn't you have a question for me? What was it? Still keeping me in suspense, are you?"

"Oh. Sorry about that, Seymour T. Seagull. Right! I did want to know about the humans. What do they look like? Why do they leave trash behind that can hurt others? Is the trash a sort of a trap for them to catch food?"

"Whoa! Hoa-be-doe-be-lo-be-ton, I thought you had only one question.

But, okay. To attempt answering you, I'll start by telling you that humans are very strange looking. They are big, ugly, clumsy, slow moving creatures. No feathers, poor things, just a pitiful fringe of fur atop their big, round heads. I've seen quite a few try to swim on top of the waves, using a long, flat stick, but they seem to fall most of the time, and then, those crazy creatures get right back on that flimsy thing, and do it again. If you ask me, I think they are crazy lunatics. But in their machines, they do get around. They're everywhere, in the air, under water, but mostly on land. But if you asked me whether they are cruel or kind, all I can tell you there is that they are all different. You can never predict how they will act. So, you got to be careful.

"Some of them are very decent, especially the ones who toss me a few good morsels to eat now and then. But many others are careless and don't seem to know all the damage they create in their wake. I've seen them ride huge, monstrous contraptions way out at sea, then get into accidents that cause huge amounts of black, sticky, poisonous gunk to spill out, killing thousands of fish and animals nearby. Still others toss lots of garbage into the water, that looks just like food to unsuspecting animals. I saw one poor old sea turtle suffocate and finally die after it ate a small, round, translucent thing that looked just like a jellyfish."

"How terrible," Lacy groaned. "How can the humans not know? And to think! You almost died too! Is their eyesight poor?"

"They can see alright. For some reason, as many amazing things as these humans are able to do, they win first place among all species for making the most mistakes, small and big. Crazy lunatics! That's what they are, and yet, I must be nearly as crazy as them, because for some reason, I've come to like them more than hate them."

"Why?" Lacy was puzzled. "They nearly killed you."

"I know. I know. I'm a ding-dang-fool, Lacy Luna, but then, through all my years of living, I've seen so many humans try to correct their mistakes, try to rescue animals and fellow humans, even when they put their own lives at great risk."

Lacy remembered Mother Whale's experience and nodded slowly.

34

Beer

Jumb

"You're not a fool, Seymour T. Seagull, not to me, anyhow. Humans just have a lot to learn, and so do I."

"Well, that makes ding-dang-donged-doodlely-do-be-do two of us." Seymour T. Seagull started flapping his wings and hopping around.

"Well," Lacy said as she crawled out of the water, and started bobbing up and down, "I'll be doggedly-dingey and a whole lot of loony too, 'cause you're indubitably correct: that makes two of us."

The two of them started dancing a silly little jig as only a seagull and crab can do together, but it came to an abrupt end. They stopped when they both heard the cry of seagulls overhead. Seymour T. Seagull looked up. "Yikes! It's my buddies. Quick, Lacy Luna! Hide in that pool now. They would think nothing of fighting over you for lunch. We, seagulls have quite an appetite, and we are particularly fond of crabmeat. I confess, I had considered eating you, but I'd be a ding-dang-dumb fool if I did. I'd rather have you as a friend, than a meal, any day! Wait, Lacy! One more thing! Take this," he said hastily as he plucked a small downy feather from his chest. He leaned over towards her outstretched claw and gave it to her. "If you wear this, I'll always know its you. I don't want to eat you by mistake!"

"Thanks," she called out to him as he took off into the air to meet his friends. She gasped in amazement as she watched him take to flight. "So graceful and free," she thought to herself, "like the bat rays of the sky." She listened as they carried on a conversation of squawks and abbreviated cries, and thought she heard Seymour T. Seagull warning them not to go down to where she was hiding. "Just a bunch of trashy rings down there." His voice trailed off as the birds flew away.

37

Camouflage

It was an early, warm afternoon when Lacy suddenly felt inspired to start decorating herself full-out. She planned to leave one bare spot near the center of her carapace for her barnacle as soon as she could find it again. But in the meantime, there was so much to explore in this particular tide pool that was teeming with life in its most brilliant colors. Bright purple sea urchins, feathery white-tipped red snails called nudibranchs, spiky pale green sea anemones, pinkish purple chitons that glided ever so slowly across encrusting algae, and lots of tiny hermit crabs that were even smaller than Lacy. There was also plenty to eat here, lime green sea lettuce, deep red algae, more near the surface of the tide pool, and then dark green algae in the deeper places.

"Where do I begin?" Lacy looked around thoughtfully and then caught sight of very teeny, hot pink strawberry anemones. "That's what I want!" She crawled close and whispered softly to them, "Would you like to live on me? I promise to take care of you."

They waved their tiny tentacles in the water in such a friendly way, she was sure they were saying "Yes!" So, with great care she picked some and placed each one as a border just above her eyes and tucked in bits of red and green algae between each strawberry anemone. Next she weaved in the otter hairs like thin braid around her wreath-like headdress. Along the center of her carapace, she planted some delicately feathered hydroids, and soft pink sponges.

She carefully tucked in the downy white feather from Seymour T. Seagull, between the feathered hydroids. She paused from her work, looked around to see what else she might add to her headdress, and then decided on just a little more red algae. As she headed back towards the surface of the tide pool, something shiny caught her attention. She crawled towards the object, and wondered what it was.

It was a quarter her size, had a flat surface, yet its shape was unusual. It had two symmetrical curves that met at a single point at the very tip, or was it the base? She wasn't sure. She touched it gingerly, wondering if it was alive, or was it a piece of dangerous trash left by a human? Nothing happened. She pushed it gently with her claw towards a patch of sunlight in the water. It glistened a bright silvery color in the light. It was one of the most exquisite things she had ever seen. "What are you?" She wondered. "Do you grow?" She watched it curiously to see if it would do anything, but it sat serenely among the thick beds of red algae. Finally she reached for it, and carefully placed it in the very center of her carapace. "If I could only find my barnacle," she sighed, thinking fondly of Mother Whale and Vibrato. She crawled on a little further along the algae patch and began to pick some to eat, when suddenly she felt something hit her claw. She stepped back.

"That's mine!" A voice shot out aggressively. The voice came from…from another decorator crab! A male, just a little bit bigger than she was.

"Oh!" Lacy said in surprise. "I'm so sorry. I didn't see you!"

"Of course not," he said abruptly. "I'm camouflaged, unlike you." He looked at her with contempt.

"Camouflage," she repeated slowly trying hard to remember its purpose.

"You don't even know what it means, do you?"

Lacy felt hot with embarrassment. She looked down, but said nothing.

"Just what I suspected. You've got a lot to learn about the right and proper way for decorator crabs to live. You should have known since birth, but no doubt you are a defect," he continued coolly.

The heat of embarrassment suddenly changed to anger, but Lacy held her tongue. Instead, she lifted herself up proudly, turned her back on him and moved away from him with as much dignity as she could muster.

"Wait! Look. I'm sorry I called you a 'defect,' but, well, what I mean is…"

Lacy turned around quickly on him and shot out, "I don't even care to know what you mean, thank you very much."

"Perhaps you don't care to know what I mean, but out of a sense of duty, I will tell you what camouflage means, so, maybe, you will be able to live longer."

Lacy felt as if there was a tug-of-war going on inside of her. A part of her did not want anything to do with this insulting creature, yet another part of her realized that at least this mean, tough crab cared at least a little about her welfare. "I'm listening," she said at last.

"Where do I begin? There is so much you need to know. I suppose I better set you straight on one of your silly notions about 'the sweetness of life' that you sang about a couple of nights ago."

"You heard me? How?"

"How else? The tides brought me to the place you used to live, and somehow, took mercy on you, feeling it was necessary to have me follow you here to this tide pool."

"Mercy on me? To have you follow me here?" Lacy's anger was growing hot once again.

"Just listen to me, girl. You want to live long, don't you?"

"My name is not 'Girl,' its Lacy, for your information."

"Okay. Lacy."

"And your name, please?"

"Leo. Pay attention now. It's for your own good."

"I'm listening," she said impatiently.

Leo paused for a while, as if thinking about the best way to teach Lacy. He looked at Lacy with a fierce intensity and then began his speech, which came out more as a syncopated chant.

"The truth about life is that
It ain't sweet.
It's full of constant dangers that
You're gonna meet.
It's a fish-eat-fish world
Out to fill its own needs,

Hurting without care
Till your heart bleeds.
The truth about life is that
It ain't sweet.
If you don't pay attention,
Then you're gonna be meat.
Listen to your instincts
That tell you to hide.
Camouflage yourself,
That's the rule to abide.
Don't stand out as different,
Instead, look the same.
Be cool. Act like others.
That's how you win the game.
You're a decorator crab,
Camouflage is your guide.
Follow it with care
If you want to survive."

Lacy was trembling with confusion by the time he finished. She wasn't sure how to respond. She looked away from his gaze. His way of living was so contrary to the way she had come to live. She considered all the dear friends she had made, but realized that each one, Mother Whale, Vibrato, Sierra, Fronda, Bobby, and Seymour T. Seagull, could have taken her life. She had taken a big risk, yet she trusted them. Or was it that she trusted her own instincts? Had she been foolish? Had she made a mistake befriending the other animals?

"Look, Lacy. I know this is tough for you. I couldn't help but notice how you danced with that seagull the other day. What a crazy, fool thing to do! And that seagull! He must have been as crazy as you, not to eat you! But do you honestly believe all seagulls will treat you the same?"

Lacy looked at the ground, more and more confused, but said nothing.

43

"Come on, Lacy. Look at me. Look at my left claw. What do you see? Tell me."

Lacy looked carefully. "It's smaller than your right," she said softly.

"That's right. I have been attacked so many times for my own foolishness. Instead of remaining hidden, instead of taking the time to camouflage myself, I went out to explore life a bit and ended up having my whole claw bitten off by a bat ray! I was just lucky I escaped, but now I've got to wait until it grows back before I look decent again."

"I'm sorry that happened to you," Lacy said sympathetically.

Leo was about to say something, but was distracted by a nearby squabble. Both he and Lacy turned their attention to small hermit crabs just below them.

Lacy looked with dismay as she saw the two tiny hermit crabs about to fight over an empty turban shell. She looked around quickly, and saw just what she needed. She grabbed it and jumped in between the two hermit crabs. "Look! See? I found another empty turban shell. It looks about the same size as the one you both want. Here," she said anxiously. "Now you can both have your own."

The two hermit crabs scurried off with their new homes just as an octopus appeared to investigate what all the commotion was about. Leo grabbed Lacy and pulled her in a deep, narrow crevice in the rock. "Be still," he hissed. The two of them watched as the octopus, with its keen eyes suddenly spotted an unsuspecting sculpin fish, captured it with one of its sucker-filled arms, and returned to its lair with its prey.

"The truth about life is that, it ain't sweet. If you don't pay attention, then you're gonna be meat," Leo reminded.

Lacy shook with fear. She was still grappling between the valuable lessons her friends taught her, and what she had just learned from Leo and the octopus. She felt as if her whole foundation of hopes and beliefs was crumbling underneath her.

"Lacy, that was kind of you to help those two hermit crabs, but it nearly cost you your life. And do you think those two crabs even appreciated what you did? Huh! They didn't even thank you. So. What good did it really do you?"

Lacy continued to be silent. She was grateful to Leo for teaching her about the purpose of camouflage, and caring about her enough to save her life, and yet, she felt as if her spirit was about to break.

"Umm. Well, I, uh, have something for you that may cheer you up. I'll be right back." In a few moments, Leo returned. "When the high waters came the other day and took us from our former home, I knew that for some reason you liked that old, abandoned barnacle, so I grabbed it just before the water grabbed me. I thought that, if there was some chance that we were dumped in the same tide pool, well, I could…you know, give it back to you."

Lacy leaned close to him and gave him a small kiss on his algae lined forehead. For a moment, it seemed that the algae turned a brighter shade of red. She wasn't sure. "Thank you, Leo," she said as she took the old barnacle from him and held it close to her. She wished right then and there she could crawl inside, and be right next to her Mother Whale. She wished she could hear her voice singing to her once more. She closed her eyes and just then she heard voices high above them. She looked up and saw two humans walking towards their pool! Leo recoiled into the deep shadows. Lacy started to follow him, but stopped short, curiosity getting the best of her. She peered out to get a better look at them but remained perfectly motionless.

"I lost it somewhere around here, I think," said the smaller of the two humans. "I wish it didn't break. I don't know how it happened. Mom's gonna be upset. She just got that for my birthday."

"Don't worry, Grace. We'll find it."

"But what if we can't find it, David?"

"That's easy. Mom or I can just get you another one for your ninth birthday. That's all."

Grace gave David a pleading look.

"Don't worry. We'll find it somehow." David looked around. "There seems to be more trash here today than there was here two days ago. I don't know why people have to litter."

"You remembered the trash bags, didn't you?"

"Yep. I got them right here." He pointed to his left thigh. "I stuffed them

45

in my pants' pocket. Okay, let's get started. Want me to check those tide pools over there?" he asked pointing.

Grace nodded. She carefully searched all around the tide pool that Lacy and Leo were in. Lacy stared in amazement at the strange looking girl. She had long strands of thick, shiny hair, like the baleen of whales, only instead of hanging from inside her mouth, it was hanging lose from the top of her head. But this girl was wearing something that looked something like camouflage, all around her head. As the girl leaned over to search the ground, and around the pool, Lacy stretched towards her to have a closer look. Just above the girl's eyes, Lacy saw small, round, bright pink things that looked just like her own strawberry sea anemones. Tucked between each bright pink sea anemone were red and green ruffles that resembled the algae.

"Ooh! A seagull's feather!" the girl said with delight. She picked it up and stuck it between the anemone and algae around her head. Lacy wondered if the feather was one of Seymour's. The girl continued to look around the pool, and as she did, she began to sing one of the sweetest songs Lacy had ever heard.

> *"Love, joy, peace, great faith, and patience,*
> *compassion, mercy, gentleness, and truth.*
> *If these virtues, you and I would follow,*
> *There would be no need of rules.*
> *Love would reign forever and ever.*
> *Peace would guide us, through and through.*
> *Love would reign forever and ever.*
> *Peace would guide us through and through."*

Lacy closed her eyes in delight. She felt as though Mother Whale was singing right to her as Grace repeated the verses over and over again until something seemed to startle her. Lacy opened her eyes and realized that this human girl, Grace, was staring right at her.

"David! Come look! Quick! I found my heart!"

"Where?" David came over to Grace's side and peered down into the tide pool where Grace was pointing. David gave a quick gasp. "How strange." David looked over at Grace, then at Lacy, and then, looked back at Grace. "Why, that's a decorator crab! It seems to be wearing a flowered hair band just like yours!"

"Yeah! That's what I noticed too. She's even wearing a feather!"

"And there's your heart, right there! He's wearing it in the center."

"That's not a boy! It's got to be a girl."

"How do you know?"

"I don't know how I know, but I just know it is."

"Well. I can catch it, and get your heart charm back, if…you want me to."

"I wish we could take her home with us. She's so cute."

"Grace. We can't do that, you know. She would die if we took her from her natural habitat. This is her home, where all her friends live."

"Yeah," Grace agreed reluctantly.

"Do you want me to get the heart from her?"

"No. I think she needs it more than I do," Grace smiled down at Lacy. Then she started to laugh. Her laughter almost sounded like music, but carried the most joyful sound Lacy had ever heard.

Then David began to laugh with her. "You're probably right." The two of them stooped down to get a closer look at Lacy, while David started explaining how and why decorator crabs camouflage themselves. Then the two of them stretched their legs.

"Well, it's time to get started cleaning up all this trash around here."

Lacy wished the two of them could somehow know that she was smiling back up at them as they walked slowly away. They not only gave her the heart, but they filled it with hope. Dragging her barnacle with her, she crawled as close as she could to get a view of the vast ocean. The bright orange sun was melting in the dazzling pink and orange water. As Lacy looked out, she was surprised to hear a faint voice call out to her to get her attention. She looked down. It was a tiny hermit crab. "Thanks for finding me a new home to wear." Lacy nodded as she watched it trail off to find some food.

The sun finally disappeared into the horizon. The sky was a blazing red color. Leo cautiously came out of his hiding place and crawled next to Lacy. She looked at him, and then back at the glowing sun. "I wonder. It seems that as different as we all may be, we are not so different from each other."

"I guess," he stammered. "I suppose we could…um. What I'm trying to say is, that…we could learn a lot from each other."

Lacy grinned in the way only crabs can. She looked at the old barnacle carefully. "I think I'm big enough to wear it now," she said, attaching it to her carapace like a crown, right behind her heart.

"Maybe you could help me find another one for me to wear," Leo suggested.

"I know just where to get you one. You might have to wait a few more months. Then, I can finally introduce you to my mother. I didn't tell you, but I am actually a whale-otter crab." She smiled at Leo who looked a little bit uneasy. If she could have laughed like Grace, she would have.

If we could create beauty with our lives

and make this holy act of living a law

as undefiable as gravity;

If we could create beauty with our lives

and become everything we aspire to be,

with all that we are inside,

then a positive force could naturally spring

into action

with the ability to heal all our wounds

earth wide.

ABOUT THE AUTHOR

Loretta Halter was born in 1957 and raised in Burbank, California. Her parents brought her up with her three brothers and two sisters in an atmosphere of love and support, and with a passion for music and dance. Loretta studied ballet, and later tap dance and jazz, until junior high. In high school she took up modern dance. Years later she studied modern dance, ballet and jazz at Cabrillo Community College in Soquel, CA, and then at San Jose State University. She earned her B.A. in Creative Arts and her state teaching credential at SJSU. While earning her credential, she took courses in biology and a course in ecology for children. These classes deepened her appreciation for nature, so that she felt it imperative to become an environmentally-based school teacher.

For the last twelve years she has been integrating the arts, science, and ecology into her lessons with fourth, fifth, and sixth graders in a San Jose public school. Inspired by the forests of the Santa Cruz Mountains, where she lives with her husband, J.T. Osgood, she has written other environmental stories, and is currently writing a sequel to *Lacy's Journey*.

ABOUT THE MUSICIAN & COMPOSER

Steve Halter is the eldest brother of the author, born in Pennsylvania in 1950, but raised in Burbank. Under the tutelage of his mother, he started learning how to play the piano at age seven. Later, in junior high, he took up guitar lessons for six months under jazz guitarist, Ron Carr. He practiced long hours and became skilled at playing both guitar and synthesizer. He became a part of the first high school rock band at John Burroughs High, called Iago, yet his heart was more drawn to folk music. After graduating from high school, he continued to hone his skills as a guitarist. Later, he and his wife Aleta had two children and raised them in a home filled with art and music. While supporting his family through day jobs, he continued to perform with several bands in the evenings.

Steve was influenced by Aleta's environmental zeal, so the two of them became involved as animal rights activists. Later, by 1995, he produced a tape of his music called *Create and Appreciate,* based on his belief that "...we're here to create and appreciate, and that success is enjoying every moment of our experience."